This book belongs to:

....

....

Bright Sparks books have been created
with the help of experts in early childhood education.
They are designed to help young children achieve
success in their early learning years.

Retold by Monica Hughes
Illustrated by Priscilla Lamont

Reading consultants: Betty Root and Monica Hughes

First published by Parragon in 2007

Parragon
Queen Street House
4 Queen Street
Bath BA1 1HE, UK

ISBN 978-1-4054-9087-0
Printed in China

The Princess and the Pea

Bath New York Singapore Hong Kong Cologne Delhi Melbourne

Helping your child read

Bright Sparks readers are closely linked to recognized learning strategies. Their vocabulary has been carefully selected from word lists recommended by educational experts.

Read the story

Read the story
to your child
a few times.

The prince opened the door, and there stood a girl.
"I am a princess," said the girl.
The girl was beautiful and wore a crown.
But she was very wet!
The prince liked the girl. But the queen said, "I will see if she is a real princess."

16

Follow your finger

Run your finger under
the text as you read.
Soon your child will begin to
follow the words with you.

Look at the pictures
Talk about the pictures. They will
help your child understand the story.

"I am a princess."

Give it a try
Let your child try
reading the large
type on each
right-hand page.
It repeats a line
from the story.

Join in
When your child is ready,
encourage him or her to join in with
the main story text. Shared reading
is the first step to reading alone.

Once upon a time there was a lonely prince.
"You would not be lonely if you got married," said the queen.

But the prince didn't want to marry just anyone.
"I want to marry a princess," he said.

"I want to marry a princess."

9

The next day he went to look for
a princess.
He saw beautiful girls.
He saw girls who wore crowns.
But they were not real princesses.

He went to look for a princess.

The prince went back to see the queen.
He told her about the beautiful girls
and the girls who wore crowns.
He told the queen that they were not
real princesses.

The prince could not find a princess to
marry.
So he was still lonely.

The prince could not find
a princess.

That night there was a big storm.
There was thunder and lightning.
Then it rained and rained and rained.

In the middle of the night there was a
knock at the door.

There was a big storm.

The prince opened the door, and there
stood a girl.
"I am a princess," said the girl.
The girl was beautiful and wore
a crown.
But she was very wet!
The prince liked the
girl. But the queen
said, "I will see if
she is a real
princess."

"I am a princess."

So the queen got a hard, dried pea.
She made a bed for the princess.
The queen put the pea under the
mattress.
She put twenty mattresses on the bed.
She put twenty quilts on the bed.

The queen put the pea
under the mattress.

"This is your bed," the queen said to the princess.

The princess had never seen a bed with twenty mattresses and twenty quilts.

The princess got into bed.

"Good night," she said to the queen.

The princess got into bed.

But the princess could not sleep.
She was awake all night.

In the morning the queen came to see
the princess.
"Did you sleep well?" asked the queen.
"No, I was awake all night," said the
princess. "There was something hard in
the bed."

The princess could not sleep.

The queen went to see the prince.
"She is a real princess," said the queen.
"She felt the pea under twenty
mattresses and twenty quilts.
Only a real princess could do that."

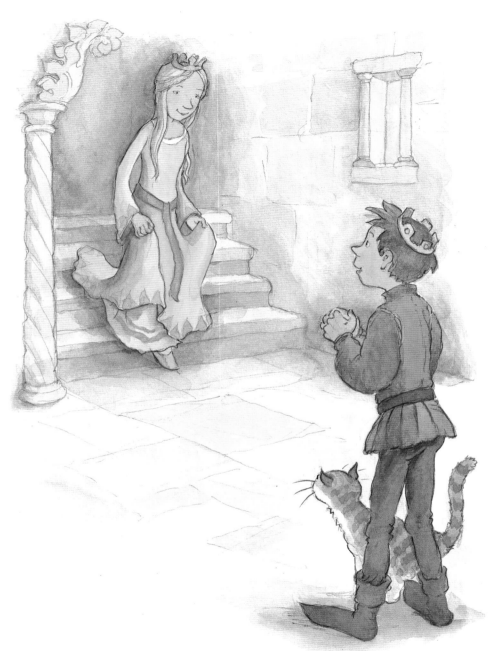

"She is a real princess."

At last the prince had found a real
princess.
"Will you marry me?" he asked.
"Yes!" said the princess.
They were married the next day.
The prince was never lonely again, and
they all lived happily ever after.

"Will you marry me?"

Look back in your book.

Can you read these words?

prince

pea

queen

mattress

princess

Can you answer these questions?

Who came to the
door in the middle
of the storm?

What did the
queen put under
the mattress?

Who did the
prince marry?

The End